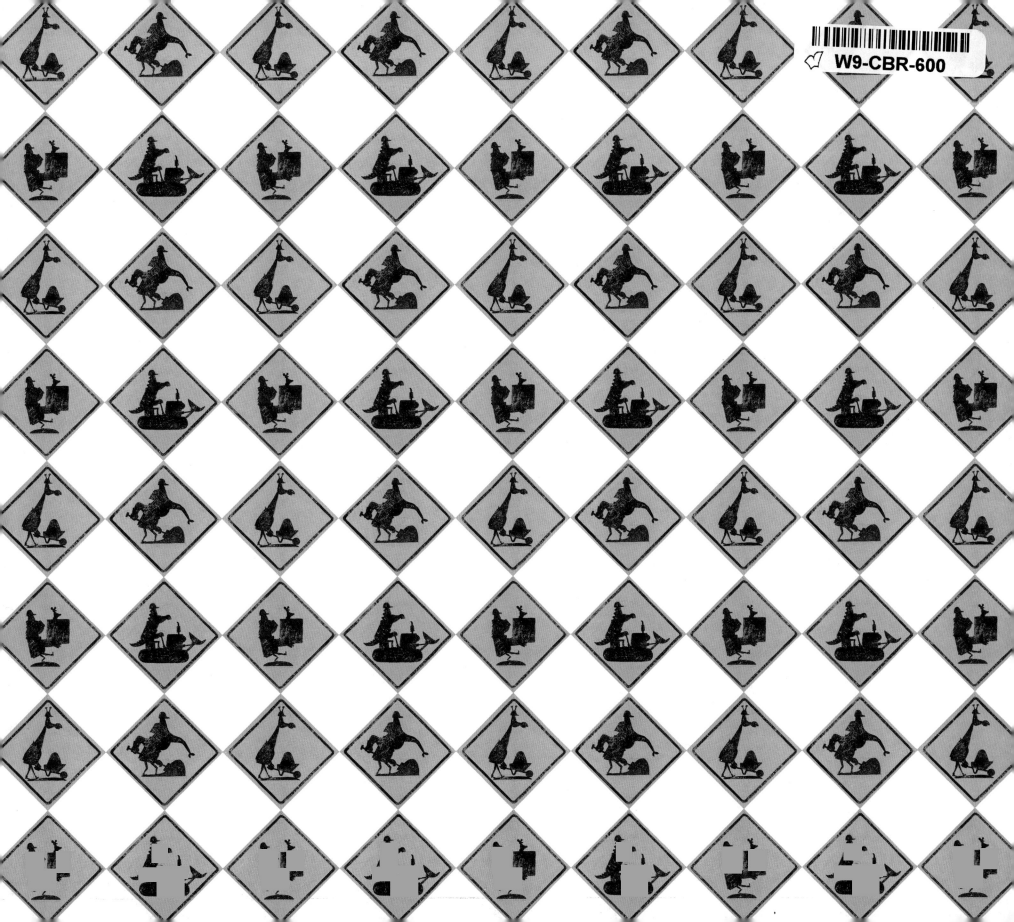

To my busiest builder and book lover, LMYKW —J. R.

For my dear friend Filip —L. T.

First published in the United States of America in June 2016
by Bloomsbury Children's Books
www.bloomsbury.com

Bloomsbury is a registered trademark of Bloomsbury Publishing Plc

For information about permission to reproduce selections from this book, write to
Permissions, Bloomsbury Children's Books, 1385 Broadway, New York, New York 10018
Bloomsbury books may be purchased for business or promotional use. For information on bulk purchases
please contact Macmillan Corporate and Premium Sales Department at specialmarkets@macmillan.com

Library of Congress Cataloging-in-Publication Data
Names: Reidy, Jean. | Timmers, Leo, illustrator.
Title: Busy builders, busy week! / by Jean Reidy ; illustrated by Leo Timmers.
Description: New York : Bloomsbury Children's Books, 2016.
Summary: A cast of animal characters are building a brand new playground in a local park and each day of the week contains a different construction plan. The construction
project comes together for a rhyming walking tour of a neighborhood, where young readers can learn the days of the week while watching everyone work as a team!
Identifiers: LCCN 2015022806
ISBN 978-1-61963-556-2 (hardcover) • ISBN 978-1-68119-029-7 (board)
Subjects: | CYAC: Stories in rhyme. | Days—Fiction. | Building—Fiction. | Playgrounds—Fiction. | Neighborhoods—Fiction. | Animals—Fiction. |
BISAC: JUVENILE FICTION / Transportation / Cars & Trucks. | JUVENILE FICTION / Concepts / Date & Time. | JUVENILE FICTION / Animals / General.
Classification: LCC PZ8.3.R2676 Bu 2016 | | DDC [E]—dc23
LC record available at http://lccn.loc.gov/2015022806

Art created with acrylic paint on paper
Typeset in Rockwell
Book design by Colleen Andrews
Printed in China by Leo Paper Products, Heshan, Guangdong
2 4 6 8 10 9 7 5 3 1

All papers used by Bloomsbury Publishing, Inc., are natural, recyclable products
made from wood grown in well-managed forests. The manufacturing processes
conform to the environmental regulations of the country of origin.

BUSY BUILDERS, BUSY WEEK!

Jean Reidy

illustrated by

Leo Timmers

BLOOMSBURY

NEW YORK LONDON OXFORD NEW DELHI SYDNEY

Sunday! Dream day!
Study, scribble, scheme day.
Map, measure, plan a treasure.
Gather up a team day!

Monday! 'Doze it day!
Dig it, dump, dispose it day.

Roll, mash, crunch, crash.
Smooth the highs and lows it day.

Tuesday! Mix day!

Pipes and boards and bricks day.

Stack, spin, pour it in.

Give the fence a fix day.

Wednesday! Load day!
Take it on the road day.

Hoist, haul, pull it all.

Something . . .

. . . being towed day!

Thursday! Fill it day!

Build it, nail it, drill it day.

Rake, spread, till a bed.

Scoop it up and spill it day.

Friday! Last day!
Pots and plants and grass day.

Scrub! Sand! Paint it grand!
Gotta finish fast day!

Saturday! Hey! Hey!
Smiles? Check! Step this way!
Finished? Yes! Take a guess!

Playtime fun for
EVERY DAY!